The
Firefighter's
Kitten

Other titles by Holly Webb

The Firefighter's Kitten

Holly Webb
Illustrated by Sophy Williams

LiTTLE TiGER

LONDON

For Martha

LITTLE TIGER
An imprint of Little Tiger Press Limited
1 Coda Studios, 189 Munster Road, London SW6 6AW

Imported into the EEA by Penguin Random House Ireland,
Morrison Chambers, 32 Nassau Street, Dublin D02 YH68

www.littletiger.co.uk

A paperback original
First published in Great Britain in 2024

Text copyright © Holly Webb, 2024
Illustrations copyright © Sophy Williams, 2024
Author photograph © Charlotte Knee Photography

ISBN: 978-1-78895-648-2

MIX
Paper | Supporting
responsible forestry
FSC® C171272

The Forest Stewardship Council® (FSC®) is a global, not-for-profit
organization dedicated to the promotion of responsible forest management
worldwide. FSC defines standards based on agreed principles for
responsible forest stewardship that are supported by environmental, social,
and economic stakeholders. To learn more, visit www.fsc.org

10 9 8 7 6 5 4 3 2 1

Chapter One

Lola sat on the stairs, looking down
at the piles and piles of boxes all over
the hallway. Somewhere in that pile
was her bedroom – or at least, all the
special things that would make the
new room at the top of the stairs hers.
Right now, that room was empty and
painted a horrid, sickly pink. But Mum
and Dad had promised they'd repaint

it soon – once they were unpacked and "organized", as Mum put it. Looking at the sea of boxes, Lola thought organized might be a long time coming.

"Are you OK up there?" Dad called, smiling up at her.

"It's all a bit strange, isn't it? I know it doesn't feel like our house yet, Lola, but I promise it will soon."

"Can I come and help?" Lola asked hopefully. "Mum said to stay here for a bit because the movers were putting boxes in the living room but they've finished now, haven't they?"

"Yes, I think they'll be gone soon," Dad agreed. "I was just putting your mum's flower pots out in the back garden. There's a couple more to carry."

Lola jumped up eagerly. There were lots of things worrying her about their new house, things that were more important than the weird pink paint – like being further away from Gran and Grandad, and not having a park anywhere close and, worst of all, starting a new school in a couple of days where she didn't know a single person. But there was *one* very good thing.

Now they had a garden.

At their old house, they'd lived in a flat, on the top floor. It had a little balcony where Mum kept all those flower pots, but the garden had belonged to the people on the ground floor. Now they had a garden all of their own.

A couple of months ago, Mum and Dad sat down with Lola and explained to her that Mum had got a new job – a really good new posting where she'd be a crew manager, but at a different fire station, which was a long way away. They told her that they needed to move house but Mum was going to be earning more, so they could have a house all to themselves and their own garden.

"We've found a lovely place," Mum said, showing Lola a photo on her phone. It just looked like an ordinary house, Lola thought, staring blankly back at her. "It's on a really quiet road. So…" She smiled, but Lola couldn't understand what she was trying to say. "You know we've always said we couldn't have a cat, not with the road here being so busy. The new house will be perfect for a cat, once we've settled in…"

Lola had the feeling they wanted her to be more excited. And she *was* excited, she really was. But it was hard to balance an imaginary cat that they *might* get one day, with a new school she was definitely going to. With new people. Away from all the friends she already had.

Still. It *was* nice to have a garden,

she thought, as she carried the pot with Mum's mint plant through the kitchen and set it carefully outside on the little patio. There was a huge lavender bush in the flower bed and the flowers were spilling over on to the sun-warmed bricks. They smelled sharp and sweet at the same time, and slow furry bees were buzzing all around. It was a beautiful place.

"I can just imagine working out here on a nice day," Dad said, slumping on to the garden bench with a happy sigh.

"Isn't it great?" Mum agreed, stepping outside behind them. "I've just found the kettle!" she added, handing Dad a cup of tea and taking a big sip from her own mug. "And the bag we packed with everything you need for Monday, Lola."

Lola nodded. She supposed that was good. She definitely didn't want to turn up for her first day at her new school in jeans. But at least she was starting at the beginning of term, even if she was going into Year Five. They'd been lucky they were able to move here just in time – for a while Mum had thought they might need to stay in a hotel for a couple of weeks.

Mum went back inside and brought out a glass of apple juice. Lola perched on the arm of the bench and leaned against Mum, slowly sipping her drink. She was so proud of her mum, getting her big new job. That was the important thing. School would be fine. Everything was going to be fine.

"Hey! Hello! Are you new?"

Lola shot a panicky look up at Dad and turned around slowly. They'd only got halfway down the road – she hadn't expected anyone to ask her that just yet.

A boy with curly dark hair was waving and running after them. "Hi!" he panted. "Are you from number twenty-seven? We saw your moving lorry on Saturday!"

"Yes…" Lola said, her voice just above a whisper. The boy seemed really friendly. She tried to smile at him but she couldn't think of anything else to say.

"What year are you in? You've got a Lark Lane jumper on. I'm in Year Five."

"Oh! Yes, me too." Lola nodded. "My teacher's Mrs Tarrant? But I haven't met her yet…"

"She's nice, we had a day with her at the end of last year," the boy explained. "I'm Noah."

"Lola. And this is my dad," Lola added, suddenly realizing that Dad was watching them both, grinning.

"It's nice to meet you, Noah," Dad said. He glanced at his watch. "We'd better keep walking, Lola. You don't want to be late on your first day."

"I'll show you a shortcut, if you like," Noah said, walking on ahead and nodding towards a little path. "Then we'll be there in loads of time. Oh look, it's Trevor!" He crouched down next to an enormous, fluffy ginger cat who was sitting in the middle of the path, guarding the way.

"Trevor!" Lola couldn't help grinning.

"Don't you think he looks like a Trevor?" Noah tickled the huge cat under his chin. "He belongs to the people in the house next to the path but he's really friendly and he's always hanging out here."

Trevor stood up and paced slowly over to Lola and Dad. He sniffed Lola's shoes and then stood in front of her, his fluffy tail standing up like a flag.

"Hello…" Lola whispered. "Will he let me stroke him?" she asked Noah.

"I don't think you'll get past him if you don't," Noah said, shaking his head. "It's definitely his path and I think he likes you."

"You're so lovely," Lola told the huge cat as she ran her hand over his ginger-striped back and then tickled his creamy chin. "Such a beautiful big boy."

"Trevor's so big, he's about the same size as all three of our cats put together," Noah said.

"You've got three cats?" Lola looked at him in surprise. "Wow, you're so lucky. We might be getting a cat, once we've got everything unpacked. Mum said there was a shelter not far away."

"Yeah, that's where we got our cats

last year." Noah nodded. "We'd better get going, I suppose," he added. "The school's just down the end of the path and along the road a bit. I'll show you."

They gave Trevor a few last pats and hurried along the path and round the corner towards the school. Lola could feel herself slowing down as they came to the gates. She didn't want to say goodbye to Dad and see him walk away.

"Mrs Tarrant's over there." Noah pointed to a teacher standing close to the doors, talking to a couple of younger girls. Lola swallowed, telling herself that Mrs Tarrant looked friendly. The teacher was smiling and waving her hands about as though she was telling some sort of funny story.

"Thanks for showing us the way, Noah. It was really kind." Dad sounded relieved – he hadn't known exactly where to go either, Lola realized.

"Noah!" Mrs Tarrant waved. "Is that Lola? I noticed she'd moved on to your road – you've met each other already, that's brilliant!"

Noah led Lola and Dad over to the teacher. "I met them on the way to school," he explained.

"Hello!" Mrs Tarrant beamed at Lola and Dad. "I was planning for you to sit on Noah's table anyway, Lola, so this is perfect. Noah can show you around today."

Lola nodded, feeling relieved. Noah was friendly and he liked cats, and Mrs Tarrant seemed nice too.

"The bell's just about to go," Mrs Tarrant said. "Why don't you show Lola where to put her bag, Noah, and then if you go into the Year Five classroom, there are names on the tables so you can see where you're going to sit."

"Great," said Dad. "Now give me a hug, Lola, and I'll see you later, OK?"

Lola flung her arms round Dad's middle and hugged him tightly. Then she hurried after Noah into the school.

Chapter Two

The kitten sniffed hopefully at the abandoned crisp packet in the gutter. It smelled salty and delicious but it was empty. He wandered on along the edge of the pavement, looking for something else to eat.

No one had put any food out behind the shops for a couple of days now and he and his sisters were desperately hungry. Their mother brought them back scraps to eat but there was never enough to make them feel full. The kitten had crept out along the alleyway, hoping to find something, anything, to fill himself up. He'd found a corner of a sandwich, which was delicious, and then he'd just kept on looking – heading further away from home.

Now he wasn't exactly sure of the way back…

There was a sharp scuffling behind him and then an excited bark, and the kitten jumped round, the fur lifting all along his spine. Rushing towards him was a dog – a huge dog, all sandy fur and great, wide jaws.

The kitten streaked away as fast as he could but the dog was a lot bigger than he was, with much longer legs. Every time he looked back, the dog was closer, those jaws practically snapping on the end of his tail. There was someone chasing after the dog, shouting at it, but the dog wasn't listening. It was going to catch him!

The kitten flung himself forwards and made a wild leap at a tree growing out of the grass verge. His claws scrabbled frantically in the bark and he shot up the trunk in a series of panicked jumps. Surely the dog couldn't follow him up here? He scrambled up another few branches, just in case.

The dog stood barking at the foot of the tree until its owner came dashing up and clipped on a lead. The dog was dragged away, but it kept looking back, whining and wagging its tail, until they turned the corner of the road.

The kitten curled into the crook of a tree branch and huddled there, shaking. He'd never been so close to a dog before. And he still didn't know which way was home.

"She doesn't talk much, does she?" someone whispered, and Lola ducked her head, trying to pretend she hadn't heard. She'd tried to be friendly and chatty at break and lunch, but she couldn't think of anything exciting to say about herself. At least it was nearly home time now.

"I guess she's just shy."

"She's boring," the first voice said, and Lola hunched forwards even further.

"Shh! She'll hear you," the second girl giggled.

"Just ignore them," Noah muttered, leaning over.

"Yeah…" Lola whispered back.

She wondered if Noah wished he hadn't adopted her on the way to school. Now he was stuck looking after a boring, silent person…

Mrs Tarrant came out to the playground with the class at the end of school and followed Lola over to chat to Dad. She said nice things about Lola's maths and how polite she was, but Lola wished she'd stop talking and let them get home.

"So, how was it?" Dad asked as they headed out of the school gates at last.

"OK." Lola shrugged. She wanted to tell Dad how lonely she'd felt all day, even with Noah helpfully showing her around and telling her people's names. But she couldn't do that.

"I'm sure it'll get easier once you know a few more people," Dad said, putting an arm round her shoulders. "You know what – we could go home and look at the website for the animal shelter. See if they've got any cats looking for a new home."

Lola stared up at him, her mouth falling open. "Really?"

"Why not?" Dad grinned and they sped up, almost trotting down the little path that led to their road. As they reached the very end, where they'd seen Trevor that morning, Lola realized that Noah was dawdling along in front of them. She thought about calling out to him – but then she didn't, in case he was trying to avoid her...

Dad didn't know that she'd been

strange and silent all day, though.
"Hey, there's Noah!" he said brightly.
"Hi, Noah!" he called and Lola cringed,
wishing she could scoot back round
the corner.

Noah swung round and he was
smiling, Lola realized. He didn't look
like he was *that* fed up with her.

"Lola and I are heading home to
look at the website for the animal
shelter," Dad told him.

"You're going to get a
cat?" Noah said gleefully,
and he held up his
hand for Lola to
high-five him.

"Our own cat!" Lola
said, laughing for the
first time that day.

"Amazing." Noah sucked in a breath and glanced down the road towards his house. "I've got to run now, I've got swimming tonight. Want to come by mine tomorrow morning? We can walk to school together. If you like," he added, looking suddenly shy.

Lola stared at him for a second and then nodded. "Is that OK, Dad?"

"I suppose so…" Dad looked a bit surprised but pleased. "Yeah, sure."

"See you tomorrow!" Lola called, and Noah waved to them as he raced off home.

The kitten peered down, listening to the voices below. He wondered about mewing so they'd notice him, but he wasn't really sure about people. He'd seen a few – they came out of the back of the shops to put things in the bins, and sometimes they'd bring food, but his mother never let the kittens go anywhere near them. She'd hiss and spit at them as if they were dangerous. Sometimes, after the people had gone away, she would pick up the kittens one at a time by the scruffs of their necks and move them to another dark hiding place: behind a different bin or in a dry corner under the thick brambles by the fence. The kitten had learned to think that people were frightening.

But people weren't nearly as frightening as that dog had been. The kitten shivered, and then shivered again as the wind rattled the leaves on the branches around him and cut through his fluffy black fur. It was colder up here, he was sure of it. The dog was long gone and the street was quiet. Time to get down and work out his way back home to his mother and sisters.

Except … down was difficult. When he'd dashed up the tree, the kitten hadn't really thought about it. He'd been so scared he just went straight up, as fast as he could. Now he could see how high he was and how far *down* was, he wasn't exactly sure how he was going to manage it.

Slowly, the kitten edged his front paws forwards, clinging to the bark with his claws as tightly as he could. The tree seemed to sway and swing beneath him, and he wriggled back quickly, his ears laid flat against his head. That wasn't going to work. He padded out along the thick branch instead, wondering if there was somewhere he could jump to – the top of a fence maybe, or another tree. But after a few steps the branch narrowed and split into thin twigs that shook and wobbled underneath him. The kitten backed up hurriedly and huddled again in his safe spot between the branch and the trunk.

It was starting to rain, he realized, with a shiver. He tried to press himself tighter against the tree trunk but the fat raindrops still splashed against his fur. Soon his coat was soaked through and plastered flat

against his skin. The kitten was
trembling all over now and he let
out a miserable mew. He wanted
to go home.

Chapter Three

Mum had been a bit doubtful about
letting Lola walk to school with Noah.
She pointed out that they'd only
known him a day! Lola tried to explain
that he'd been really kind and looked
after her at school, but she insisted on
coming with Lola the next morning
– her shift didn't start until a bit later
on. She said she wanted to say hello to

Noah's parents. Luckily, Noah's mum seemed to have thought the same way, and Lola and Noah left them chatting together on Noah's front doorstep as they set off for school. One of Noah's cats was sniffing curiously at Lola's mum's shoes.

"Make sure you come straight home this afternoon, Lola," Mum called after her. "Dad will be watching out for you."

"Don't worry about what Marnie and Bella said yesterday," Noah said as Lola turned back to nod and wave. "You shouldn't listen to them. They're always saying mean stuff about people."

"I'm fine…" Lola said, trying to sound as though she meant it. She glanced around, trying to find something, anything to help her change the embarrassing subject, and then squeaked. "Oh! Look – up in that tree! Is it a kitten?"

Noah peered up too. "Wow, yeah, you're right."

Lola hurried closer. The kitten was crouched in the angle between the trunk and one of the branches, staring down at them. It looked as though it should be fluffy but its long black fur was matted with rain. "Hey…" Lola called. "Hello, kitten. Are you OK up there?"

The kitten let out a mew – so quiet that Lola could hardly hear it.

"Do you think it's all right?" she said, looking worriedly at Noah.

"I'm sure it's fine. Our cats are always climbing into weird places.

The only time we had to rescue one of them was when Soda got stuck in the window blind. They're really good at climbing trees, they always come down when they're ready."

"Oh… OK." Lola nodded. She didn't know much about cats yet, she supposed, and Noah did. But the kitten looked too small to be all the way up there.

"We'd better go," Noah said. "Your mum won't be happy if you're late for school the first day you go without her or your dad, will she?"

Lola's eyes widened. "No! OK, come on." But she kept turning back as they hurried down the path, looking at the tiny ball of black fur huddled high in the tree.

The kitten let out a loud, long wail. He was cold and hungry and miserable, and he really didn't know how to get down. He'd hated being stuck in the tree overnight. Even though his night sight was good, the darkness was full of strange noises –

scuffling and squawks, odd chattering from the birds roosting in the branches and eerie footsteps echoing from the pavement below. He'd lain there, wishing for the comfortable nest of newspapers and old cardboard that his mother had made, snuggled up with his sisters in a warm, breathing pile of fur. What if he fell asleep and then slipped out of the tree? He could feel the branch swaying with the wind, and he hated it.

"He's still up there."

The kitten leaned over the branch, looking down at the two people below.

"I was sure he'd be down by now – that's a whole day and night. He really is stuck. I'm going to get a ladder, see if we can coax him down."

The kitten watched anxiously as they hurried away. He wasn't sure what he wanted to happen. He understood that he needed someone to help him get down, but he was still suspicious, remembering his mother and her frightened hissing. When the elderly man and woman came back with a ladder and propped it up against the tree and it thumped and squeaked and creaked, he hissed too and tried to climb further up. But he was so tired and cold, and his paws kept slipping. He hunched himself down against the wet bark and closed his eyes tight. Perhaps if he couldn't see them, they'd go away.

Lola's day was going a lot better than she'd thought it would. Mrs Tarrant liked to set tasks for when everyone arrived in the morning, and today's had been to write a paragraph on something interesting about your family. Lola nearly put that they were going to get a cat but then decided that some people might not think it was exciting (they were wrong). Instead, she wrote *My mum is a firefighter and she can drive a fire engine*, and then explained that they'd moved house so her mum could be a crew manager at the local fire station.

Everyone looked impressed when she read it out, and Tierney, one of the girls who shared a table with her and Noah, told Lola at break that she really wanted to be a firefighter, and that Lola's mum sounded amazing. Tierney came and sat down next to Lola at lunchtime and Lola started to feel as if she was making another friend.

"I wonder if that little black cat's still in the tree," Lola said to Noah as they grabbed their coats at the end of school. "I kept thinking about him all day."

"He won't be," Noah said confidently. "I'm telling you."

But when they turned on to the path, there was a huge red fire engine parked at the far end and a knot of people standing around the tree.

"Maybe you were right about that kitten?" Noah said, and Lola gasped. "That's my mum!"

They wriggled their way around the edge of the crowd to the front and watched a team of firefighters propping a tall ladder up against the tree. Lola's mum waved at her and then set off up the ladder.

"That kitten must be so hungry," Noah said. "It's been up there all day."

"Longer than that," said a woman standing next to them, shading her eyes with her hand as she gazed up at the tree. "I first spotted it yesterday morning."

"Oh wow, it was in the tree all night?!" Lola gasped. "It was pouring with rain! The kitten must be freezing."

"We tried to get it to come down earlier on," the woman explained, "but our ladder wasn't long enough and the poor little thing was too scared to move. In the end I called the RSPCA, and they sent out the fire brigade."

"I hope Mum can get the kitten down," Lola said anxiously. "That's my mum up the ladder," she explained, and the woman smiled at her.

"She's very brave. I wouldn't like to climb that high."

"She is," Lola agreed. "Oh look, she's nearly got it!"

Lola's mum was leaning carefully out to the side of the ladder, so close to the shivering kitten. Lola held her breath. Would Mum be able to reach?

Chapter Four

The kitten wriggled himself back against the trunk of the tree, hissing faintly. He wanted to get down but not like this. The person was reaching for him, grabbing. He batted at them with his paw, tiny claws extended, but they didn't seem to notice.

"Got you! It's OK. Poor little thing."

He was snatched up, then tucked

away inside a thick black coat.
Terrified, the kitten stopped hissing
and froze. What was happening?
Where were they taking him?

He was out of the wind, at least,
snuggled up inside the coat. He
seemed to have been cold for as long
as he could remember – his fur had
hardly dried at all after last night's
rain. He could feel the person's heart
thumping gently – it felt a little like
being curled up against his mother and
the other kittens.

Then they stepped off the ladder
and there was a sudden rush of noise
– clapping and shouting. The kitten
gave a tiny mew of fright and wriggled.
He wasn't cuddled up with his mother
at all – the coat smelled bad, sharp

and smoky, and he didn't want to be anywhere near it. He needed to get away!

He slipped out of the grasping hands and made a wild leap for the ground, but there were people everywhere, more noise and trampling feet.

"Oh…" A quiet whisper. Hands reached out but didn't snatch. Gentle fingers ran over his fur and the kitten leaned against them in relief. "He's scared. He doesn't understand what's happening." Very carefully, two small hands cradled him and lifted him up.

"Isn't he beautiful?" Lola's mum said. "I think he'd be really fluffy if his fur

wasn't all wet. I'm honestly not sure
if he's a boy or a girl kitten, actually.
But it seems odd to keep saying 'it'."

"He must be so cold," Lola
whispered back. "I think he's shivering.
He's frightened of all the noise."

"We should give him back to his
owners now, Lola," Mum said gently,
and Lola sighed and nodded. Her
mum scanned the small crowd of
people and smiled at an elderly man.
Lola was pretty sure he lived in the
house close to the path – he might
even be Trevor's owner.

"It was you who called us out,
wasn't it? Here's your kitten back,
safe and sound."

The elderly man shook his head.
"Oh no, sorry. He's not actually mine.

We called the RSPCA because we were worried about him. He'd been up that tree since yesterday morning, poor little scrap."

"Oh…" Lola's mum frowned. "You don't know who he belongs to?"

"No idea, sorry. I've not seen him around before."

"I'm sure I'd have noticed if he belonged to someone on the street," his wife added.

There was a general chorus of agreement from the people standing around – no one knew where the kitten lived. Lola's mum went off to talk to the rest of her fire crew, perhaps to see if they had any ideas about what to do.

Lola cuddled the black kitten against her school cardigan. He was so little and thin and cold, and now it seemed like no one wanted him. If he had an owner, they hadn't bothered to come looking for him while he was stuck up that tree. "Poor little lost kitten…" she whispered, tickling him behind his ears, and the kitten rubbed his chin wearily against her hand.

"I bet he's hungry," Noah said, leaning over to look at him.

Lola nodded. "He can't have eaten anything for ages. I've got half a ham sandwich left in my lunch box, do you think he'd like that?"

"Want me to get it out?" Noah started unzipping Lola's backpack. "You were too busy talking to Tierney to finish it! Here." He lifted up the top slice of bread and pulled a sliver of ham out of the sandwich.

"See if he'll eat it," Lola said, looking hopefully at the kitten.

The kitten had been curled up against her cardigan, watching suspiciously as the firefighters put the ladder away and the crowd slowly headed back home. But he seemed to catch the smell of the ham sandwich at once. Lola felt a shiver run through him, as if he'd woken up, and he leaned out to sniff eagerly at Noah's hand. He put out a paw and touched the piece of ham curiously. Then he lunged at it, snapping it out of Noah's fingers and gobbling it down.

"Wow, he definitely wanted that," Noah murmured, pulling out another piece and offering it cautiously. "Don't you bite my fingers off…"

"He's starving," Lola said. "I wish I had something else but he isn't going to want an apple, is he?" she added

"Nope." Noah fed the last bit of ham to the black kitten and wiped his buttery fingers on his school trousers. "I could go home and get some cat food for him, though. We've got loads."

"Oh, yes!" Lola nodded eagerly. She glanced over at her mum, who was talking on the phone, explaining about the kitten and how no one knew where he belonged. "It doesn't look like he's going anywhere soon."

Noah raced off down the road and came back a couple of minutes later with a small cat bowl filled with food. Lola thought it smelled a bit disgusting but the kitten didn't seem to think so at all – as soon as Noah got near, he started to mew loudly and wriggled in Lola's hands.

"It's OK, look. There you go." Lola put him down carefully next to the bowl and the kitten began guzzling the food.

"I hope he doesn't throw up," Noah muttered.

Lola's mum ended her call and came over to look at the kitten. "Well done for getting him some food – thanks, Noah."

"What's going to happen to him, Mum?" Lola asked anxiously.

"Well, a couple of the crew checked the local websites to see if anyone had reported him missing but there's nothing about a lost kitten. I was just on the phone to the animal shelter and they're really busy. All their foster homes are full but they said they can probably find someone who can look after him tomorrow."

"But … what about now?" Lola said, looking down at the kitten licking all the way around the empty bowl, making absolutely sure he hadn't missed anything. Someone needed to take him home…

The kitten sat down rather unsteadily. He was very full. He'd never had that much to eat before, not all in one go. Slowly, he lifted up a paw and swiped it over his whiskers to catch any scraps of food. Then again, round his ears… He knew he ought to be setting out to find his mother and the nest behind the bins, but he was full and sleepy and somehow it didn't seem quite as important as it had before.

The girl who'd rescued him from the noise and shouting picked him up again carefully and wrapped the side of her cardigan around him. It was very warm and the kitten gave a massive yawn, slumping against her hand.

"He's gone all saggy," the girl whispered.

"I think he's falling asleep," murmured a boy. "Look, you can actually *see* where he ate that whole bowl of food. He's round in the middle!"

The kitten drifted off to sleep as they whispered softly over his head.

Chapter Five

"There's my dad!" Lola said, glancing up in surprise. Dad was walking down the street, looking at the fire engine, and there was a relieved expression on his face.

"Hello, Emma!" he called, waving to Lola's mum, who was on the phone again, and she waved back, pointed to Lola and then mouthed, "Sorry!" at him.

"I was getting worried about you,"
Dad said, putting his arm round Lola's
shoulders and giving her a hug. "I was
about to set off looking for you when
I spotted the fire engine."

Lola gasped. "Sorry, Dad... Mum
was here and I didn't think about you
worrying. Look, she rescued a kitten!"
Carefully, she pulled back the side
of her cardigan and showed him the
sleeping black kitten. He was definitely

getting fluffier as he dried out.

"Wow! He's tiny. Where did Mum rescue him from?"

"Up that tree." Noah pointed and Dad gave him a disbelieving look.

"That little cat? He couldn't get all the way up there."

"He did, honestly, Dad. The people who called for help said he'd been there since yesterday morning. He must have been there when we walked home yesterday, and we saw him today when we were going to school. He was stuck up there all night! I bet he was so scared." Lola ran one finger gently over the soft black fur on the kitten's head and he let out a little wheezy noise in his sleep, a noise that was almost a purr.

"He must be a lot more adventurous than he looks right now," Dad said, smiling.

"Mum's trying to find somewhere for him to go." Lola sighed. "The animal shelter's full and so are all their kitten fosterers."

"Oh." Dad looked thoughtful.

"They think they can find someone to look after him tomorrow," Lola explained. "But he's got nowhere to go tonight." She glanced at Noah. "Do you think you could look after him? You know lots about cats."

Noah shook his head sadly. "I'd love to but I don't think our cats would like it. They get on OK with each other – most of the time – but they hate it if another cat even dares to walk along our back fence. They launch out of the cat flap all fluffed up and furious. But why couldn't you take him?"

Lola blinked at him and Dad looked surprised. Noah shrugged. "You said you were going to look at cats on the shelter website last night!"

Lola nodded. "We did! There was a beautiful tabby that I liked but it said he was nervous and might not be suitable to live with children. Dad was going to send them an email asking if nine was old enough…"

"Well, here's a cat who needs looking after – and he doesn't seem nervous. Not any more, at least." Noah looked down at the kitten, who was now definitely snoring inside Lola's cardigan.

"I-I suppose so," Lola said slowly. "I just thought it needed to be somebody who knew what they were doing. Because he's so little. And Mum and Dad said we had to be settled in before we could get a cat…"

"Noah's right, though." Dad nodded. "The kitten needs somewhere, and it's only for a night, until his owner turns up or the shelter finds someone to foster him. I'm sure we can muddle through. And it *does* look as though he likes you, Lola!"

"But we haven't got a cat bed, or – or anything!" Lola said, staring worriedly down at the kitten.

"He seems to be OK in your cardigan," Dad pointed out. "We'll make do. Come on – let's check that your mum's all right with it, then we can head home before he wakes up."

Lola's mum was a bit surprised at the idea but then she nodded. "OK... To be honest, I'm not sure what else to do with him. I was just about to ring the shelter again and beg them to squeeze him in! I've got to get going – we're due back at the station now. See you later!" She hurried back on to the fire engine and it pulled away, with all the firefighters waving.

"I'll go home and ask Mum for some more cat food," Noah said helpfully. "He'll want to eat again when he wakes up. Kittens like to eat lots of small meals."

"Thanks, Noah!" Lola smiled at him gratefully.

"That would be great," Dad agreed. "I reckon we can find everything else we need at home somewhere. And we've got a houseful of cardboard boxes to make cat beds with!"

Lola laughed out loud, thinking of the towers of boxes stacked in every room of the house, and the kitten snuffled and shifted against her cardigan. "Sorry! Sorry!" she whispered. She didn't want him to wake up and try to run off again. But the little black kitten was still fast asleep.

When they got home, Dad found a smallish cardboard box and Lola carefully slid out of her cardigan, keeping it wrapped warmly around the snoozing kitten. Then they tucked the kitten and the cardigan into the box –

a perfect cat bed. Lola put the box down gently in the corner of the kitchen, where no one would trip over it.

Noah had popped over with several tins of cat food from his mum, so there was no danger of the kitten not having enough to eat.

"What about when he needs the loo?" Lola asked Dad. She was sitting on the floor next to the box and it looked as if the kitten might wake up soon. He'd definitely wriggled and yawned a couple of times. "He's eaten so much food, Dad. I think he might need a poo when he wakes up!"

Dad looked around the kitchen, frowning. "I hadn't thought about that. We need a cat litter tray. I suppose he's probably too young to be house-

trained but we should try anyway. Oh!
I know. Hang on a minute, Lola." He
unlocked the door to the patio. "Make
sure you don't let him out when I come
back in," he added, disappearing into
the garden.

Lola looked down at the kitten.
One greeny-yellow eye was opening
but he still looked sleepy. She didn't
think he was about to make a great
escape into the garden. Not just yet.

Dad came back with a grubby-looking plastic tray. "I noticed there were a few odd bits left in that little garden shed," he explained. "It's a seed tray. I'll give it a quick rinse and we can tear up some of the newspaper we used for packing. I'd better be quick," he said, eyeing the kitten, who was standing up and stretching in his cardigan nest.

By the time the kitten was properly awake, Dad had made him a perfect litter tray in a quiet, out-of-the-way corner opposite his basket. Dad lifted him into it just in time.

"You did *say* he ate a lot," he said to Lola afterwards. "I hadn't realized quite how much…"

When Mum got back from her shift later that evening, Lola and Dad were in the kitchen showing the kitten how to play with a ball of rolled-up newspaper. They'd given him a bath in the kitchen sink, which he hadn't liked that much, but Dad said they needed to in case of fleas. Lola wasn't really sure what fleas looked like but there were definitely a lot of little black specks in the water when they rinsed him off. The kitten looked even tinier when he was wet, skinny and miserable, with his long fur all sticking up in spikes. Lola had wrapped him in a soft towel and rubbed him dry, and he'd cheered up a bit after that.

"He looks happy," Mum said, sinking into one of the kitchen chairs with a sigh. "I think I can count him as a successful rescue."

The kitten shot across the kitchen tiles after the paper ball and jumped on top of it, all claws out. Then he yawned and rested his chin on the squished newspaper.

"I feel like that too," Mum said, laughing. "I think he's about to fall asleep right there!"

"Can he sleep on my bed?" Lola asked hopefully. She loved the thought of a cat sleeping on the end of her bed, or maybe even curled up next to her pillow.

"Better not," Dad said. "I know we managed to get him to poo in the litter tray but he made a puddle on the floor, remember? He's not house-trained. You don't want him to wee in your room."

"I suppose so…" Lola agreed sadly. "Night, kitten. Sleep well." She snuggled him back into his box – she'd rescued her cardigan now, and it was lined with a couple of tea towels instead, but the kitten didn't seem to notice that. He stretched out his front paws, gave a huge yawn and slumped back into sleep.

The kitten woke again a few hours later and peered uncertainly around the kitchen. He was comfortable and warm in the softly padded box, and he'd had so much to eat that he was almost not hungry. But he was all on his own. Apart from that terrifying night in the tree, he'd never slept alone before. He was used to spending the night curled up in a knot of legs and tails with his sisters. His mother would slip out to forage for food and then she'd come back and wrap herself comfortingly around her kittens to sleep away the rest of the night.

The dark, empty kitchen was horribly lonely, and the kitten let out a frightened, miserable mew, and then another, and another.

Upstairs, Lola was finding it hard to get to sleep. Too much had happened that day and she couldn't stop telling it to herself all over again. The fire engine and the soft damp fur of the kitten under her fingers. The delicious little chomping noises he'd made as he worked his way through that bowl of food there on the street.

Oh, she was never going to fall asleep! Lola sighed and turned over, thumping her head into her pillow. Then she sat up, her heart suddenly racing. Was that a mew from downstairs? She froze, listening in the darkness – there it was again! Such a sad, lonely noise. Of course the kitten would be frightened and lonely if he woke up all on his own.

Lola didn't even have to think. She was up at once, dragging the duvet off her bed and creeping out of her bedroom and along the dark landing. She could just about see in the light from the street lamp outside. Dad was right – she didn't want the kitten to accidentally wee on her bed – but that didn't mean he had to be alone downstairs. Lola tiptoed down the staircase and carefully pushed open the kitchen door to find the black kitten right in front of it like a darker patch of shadow, mewing desperately.

"It's all right! Oh, don't be so sad, little one," she murmured, scooping him up. "You need someone to look after you, don't you? Look, I'll put my duvet here next to your box." Gently she popped the kitten back into his cardboard box bed and made herself a warm nest of duvet beside him. The kitten stared at her for about half a minute and then decided that she looked a lot better than the box and clambered out to join her in the duvet.

Lola's last thought as she fell asleep was, *Wouldn't it be nice to sleep like this every night?*

Chapter Six

Lola woke up feeling stiff – the duvet on the hard kitchen floor wasn't as comfortable as a real bed. But there was a kitten curled up underneath her chin, a little ball of dark fur that was still snoring. She really didn't care about her achey muscles.

Her mum was standing by the kitchen counter waiting for the kettle to boil. "I went to wake you up for school and you weren't there!" she said, laughing.

"Sorry, Mum..." Lola said with a yawn, and the kitten sat up and yawned too, his pink wide-open mouth surprising against his black fur. "He was crying..."

Mum shook her head. "That kitten knows you're a soft touch already." She smiled at Lola and then looked at Dad, who had just walked into the kitchen. "He's going to have Lola completely wrapped around his paw in a couple of days, isn't he?"

Lola blinked at her. She was still sleepy and not absolutely sure what Mum meant. "A couple of days? But ... don't we have to take him to the animal shelter today?"

Dad sat down in the chair nearest to Lola's duvet nest. "Well… Your mum and I were talking about it last night and we realized that would be a bit silly. We were going to adopt a cat from the shelter, weren't we? And here we are with a kitten who needs a home. So, why don't we just keep him?"

Lola nodded slowly. She'd been thinking they had to take the black kitten to the shelter – that's where lost kittens *belonged*. But Dad was right. If the kitten was happy with them, and they wanted to keep him, then why shouldn't they?

"But ... but what if he belongs to someone else?" Lola whispered.

"We've already told the shelter about him," Mum reminded her. "And I put him on the local Lost and Found Pets page. If anyone's lost a kitten, they'll get in touch. But there's been nothing yet."

Lola tickled the kitten under his chin – now that he was warm and dry, he was really fluffy – and then she realized something. "If we're keeping him, then we've got to give him a name!"

"Good point," Dad agreed, leaning down to look at the kitten. "He looks like a Sooty to me."

Lola chewed her bottom lip. "Maybe…" It just wasn't quite right.

"Peter," suggested Mum, and Lola shook her head definitely.

"Mum! No! Does he *look* like a Peter?"

The kitten yawned hugely again and Lola's mum laughed. "OK, maybe not."

"I think we should call him Arlo," Lola said. She wasn't quite sure where she'd heard the name but she liked it. And she liked that it looked and sounded a little bit like Lola. If he was an Arlo, the kitten would definitely belong to her.

"Ooooh," Mum said slowly. "I like it."

Dad nodded. "Hey, Arlo," he said experimentally to the kitten, and Arlo looked up at him at once. "OK, that works!"

Arlo had slept comfortably for the rest of the night, tucked up inside the duvet next to Lola. He woke up a couple more times and gazed out into the darkness of the kitchen, but he didn't feel lonely when he could hear Lola's steady breathing and feel her warmth settling into his fur. It was almost like being back in the little nest with his sisters, except he wasn't hungry any more and there was nowhere for the rain to get in.

He missed his sisters, and his mother. But this was a good, safe place, far away from loud, scary dogs and trees that shook in the night wind. He wished his mother and sisters could be here too, safe and warm and well fed with him. He didn't think his mother would like being so close to people, though, not even when the people meant a cosy bed and such delicious food. He understood why she was so scared – he had been terrified when Lola's mother first picked him up. But now – maybe here was where he ought to stay?

Lola had tried to imagine having a cat of her own but she'd never really known what it would be like. How brilliant it was to come down in the morning and have a kitten fling himself at her feet and try to eat her socks. How much easier homework was if a kitten was asleep on her lap. How funny it would be to have a kitten sitting under the table during dinner, patting her leg with his paw every so often to remind her that he liked fishfingers too. More than Lola did, actually.

Mum and Dad loved him too. Arlo was getting much better about using the litter tray, which had been Dad's big worry – there had only been a couple of puddles to clear up. And now that Arlo was a bit more house-trained they could let him out of the kitchen. Mum loved sitting on the sofa with him when she got home from a busy shift. She said that the little black kitten's purrs were very soothing. Arlo didn't seem so worried about sleeping on his own in the kitchen any more either. Lola thought that probably meant he'd decided their house was home now, and it was safe. She hoped that soon Mum and Dad would agree that Arlo didn't need to stay in the kitchen overnight and he could come and sleep on her bed instead.

A couple of weeks after Arlo had come to live with them, Lola wandered downstairs on Saturday morning to find Dad at the kitchen table tying knots.

"What are you doing?" she asked curiously, watching as he muttered to himself.

"Oh! I didn't see you there, Lola. Sorry. I'm trying to make one of those feather dancer toys for Arlo. The ones we looked at in the pet shop were so expensive. I happened to spot a couple of feathers on the pavement when I walked back from the shops yesterday so I thought I'd have a go. It was trickier than I thought it would be – but I reckon this is ready for a first testing."

Lola inspected the feathery string that Dad had tied on to a bit of thin stick. It definitely looked like the toys in the pet shop. They'd gone there to buy Arlo a proper bed after school a couple of days before. The kitten was already much bigger than when he'd arrived at their house, and Dad said he was growing out of his box. They'd looked at cat toys too, and a cat tree, but a lot of the things were expensive. Dad said maybe Arlo could have a cat tree for Christmas. They chose a catnip fish instead and the kitten loved it. He'd spent ages rolling around on the floor, batting it between his paws and kicking at it with his hind feet. Then he'd taken it with him into his box. He hadn't quite got used to the new bed yet.

Lola glanced over at the box – now

next to the cat bed – expecting to see the fish tucked up with Arlo again. But Arlo wasn't there.

"Oh! Did he sleep in the bed at last?" she asked, pleased. They'd chosen a lovely bed, all soft and furry and shaped like a little cave, with just a hole for the cat to pop in and out. It was meant to help Arlo feel safe and secure inside, but it made it quite hard to see him. Lola peered in, expecting to see a small kitten snoozing inside. But Arlo wasn't there either.

"No, he was in the box. Your mum fed him breakfast before she left for her shift and he went back to bed to sleep it off." Dad glanced over at the box, as if he thought Lola might just have missed Arlo asleep in it. "Oh. Maybe he's in the living room. You know he likes trying to climb the cardboard boxes in there."

They were still unpacking, and the tower of cardboard boxes was going down, but very slowly. Arlo had discovered that if he sank his claws into the cardboard, the boxes made a great kitten climbing frame. Lola was thinking of suggesting they didn't bother with a cat tree and just kept the cardboard boxes instead. But Arlo wasn't halfway up any of the boxes.

He wasn't stuck in the drawer with

the tea towels, or in Lola's toy box, or any of the other dark and cosy places he liked to hide himself in. He wasn't underneath the sofa, waiting to pounce on Lola's feet. He wasn't sitting on the living room windowsill watching the cars or on the kitchen windowsill chittering at birds.

He wasn't *anywhere*.

Chapter Seven

Arlo blinked sleepily. He wasn't really sure about the new bed that had appeared next to his box. It smelled odd. Perhaps in a while he'd want to sleep in it, but not just yet. There were lots of other places to curl up and sleep in the house, though. He'd found this cosy place earlier on, small and dark and smelling of Lola's mum, and climbed in.

The problem was, it felt different now. The space still smelled good, and it was comfy, curled up inside the soft fabric, but there was a bright white light overhead, and far too much noise. Banging and slamming and shouting – it was all so loud.

The kitten burrowed himself even deeper under the hoodie inside Lola's mum's backpack, all his fur standing on end. After that, the noise seemed to die down for a while, and eventually Arlo felt brave enough to look out and see what was going on. He didn't think Lola would like all this commotion either so perhaps if he could find her, she would make it stop.

Arlo wriggled out of the warm hoodie and peered through the open zip top of the backpack. The bag was sitting on a bench in a brightly lit room filled with metal lockers, and he could hear people walking about and calling to each other in the distance. He wriggled out of the backpack and hopped quickly down on to the bench, padding along until he could see out of the open locker room door.

There was an enormous, high-ceilinged room out there, with a cold, echoing concrete floor. Arlo had never seen anything like it, and he was almost sure that this wasn't part of his house.

He'd curled up to sleep in a snug bag inside his own kitchen and now he was somewhere else entirely.

Lola and Dad had searched everywhere – even upstairs, although they didn't think Arlo had been upstairs yet. But as Dad said, there had to be a first time. It was horrible, looking inside every cardboard box and hoping that this time there would be a fluffy black kitten gazing back. But there never was.

"Do you think Arlo could have got out?" Lola asked Dad when they met in the hallway, her voice quavering. "I can't find him anywhere. I kept calling, and you know he usually comes running if we call because he thinks he's going to get treats."

"We've been so careful, checking for him every time we open the front door," Dad murmured. "But I suppose he might have done. He's so little and quick… Maybe we didn't notice… We'd better go outside and have a look."

Dad and Lola hurried up and down the street, calling Arlo's name. Lola kept ducking down to check underneath the cars, and she flinched every time a car rolled down the road, imagining Arlo running out in front of it. At least their road had speed bumps so the cars couldn't go very fast.

Dad was leaning over the garden walls, peering in and looking for a dark little kitten hidden among the plants.

Lola almost wished that Arlo was ginger. He'd be a lot easier to see.

"What are you doing?" someone asked as she crouched to look under a blue van, and Lola jumped up with a squeak.

"Don't creep up on me!" she told Noah crossly.

"I didn't! I just walked up behind you, I wasn't creeping. You weren't paying attention."

Lola sighed. "You're right, I probably wasn't."

"So, what *are* you doing?" Noah asked, leaning down to see under the car as well.

"Looking for Arlo," Lola explained. "He's disappeared. We can't find him in the house so we're checking out here."

"Oh no…" Noah darted over to look into the nearest garden. "Do you know how long ago he got out?"

"We don't even know that he *did* get out," Lola explained. "But we've looked everywhere inside. We've checked all the hiding places we can think of – he's always climbing into things. And he was definitely at the house this morning. My mum fed him before she went to the fire station."

"That's not very long," Noah said. "He can't have got far."

"I know, but there are just so many places he could be." Lola shrugged helplessly.

"What about the tree?" Noah suggested. "He went up it once."

Lola shook her head. "But he hated it! He was stuck and he was really scared." Then she sighed. "But I suppose it's worth a try." She looked back down the road and called, "Dad! We're just going to check in case he's gone up that tree again!"

Her dad nodded and waved, and Noah and Lola raced along the pavement to stare up into the huge tree.

"I can't see him," Lola said doubtfully, shading her eyes as she tried to peer between the yellowing leaves.

"Me neither," Noah said, sighing. "Oh well. I suppose that's a good thing. If he'd gone up the tree, we would have had to call your mum out all over again. I bet they wouldn't have been very happy at the fire station."

Lola nodded and then swallowed hard. "I suppose we ought to call my mum," she said slowly. "We should tell her Arlo's missing."

Arlo looked around the door of the locker room. He still wasn't sure how he'd ended up here – or how he was going to get home. But he had to try. The last couple of weeks living with Lola and Mum and Dad had felt so different to his old home behind the bins in the alley. It wasn't just that he'd had enough to eat, although that was part of it. But he'd been fussed over and stroked and played with and talked to – and he loved it. He wasn't going to stay here. The fire station was big and cold and strange and it smelled awful. He needed to find Lola again.

Cautiously, he padded out into the big, open space, wondering if Lola's mum was anywhere around. He'd been curled up in that bag, sleeping inside a hoodie that smelled of her. So perhaps she was here too? There were all sorts of strange things in the room – coats that smelled

like the one Lola's mum had been
wearing when she fetched him down
from the tree: strong and sharp, like
chemicals. Huge black boots.

He put his paws up on the edge of one and peered in, liking the look of the dark space inside. Perhaps he could hide in there… But that wouldn't help him find Lola. He looked up curiously at an enormous wheel but he didn't recognize the fire engine that had been parked underneath his hiding-place tree.

A sudden clanging alarm cut through the air, so loud that Arlo ran in panic. He had no idea where he was going, just that he needed to get away from that wild noise. A loudspeaker rattled into life above him and then there were racing footsteps and shouts. Arlo shot up the steps of the fire engine he'd been sniffing and looked around wildly for somewhere to hide.

The firefighters were pulling on
their kit and clambering into the other
fire engine. The alarm cut out at last
and the fur settled along Arlo's spine
– before blue lights shone through the
windows of the fire engine where he
was hiding, the huge metal shutter
at the front of the station rattled up,
and a siren began to shriek as the
engine roared away.

Arlo stayed
tucked under
the driver's
seat of the
second engine,
too frightened
to move.

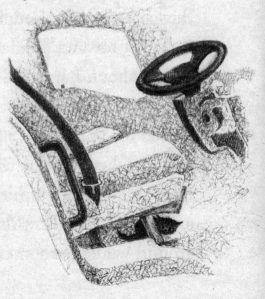

Chapter Eight

"Any sign?" Dad called, hurrying up the street towards Lola and Noah.

Lola shook her head miserably. "We should call Mum and let her know."

Dad sighed. "Yes, I suppose you're right." He pulled out his phone. "I still don't understand how Arlo could have got out. We've been so careful."

He'd just unlocked the phone screen when they spotted the neighbour who'd reported that Arlo was stuck in the tree – he was called Mr Khan and Lola had been right, he *was* Trevor's owner. They'd spoken to him a few times since then, and he loved cats.

"Here." Dad pushed his phone into Lola's hands. "You call Mum, love. I'll just go and let Mr Khan know that Arlo's missing. He and Mrs Khan can keep an eye out for us too. And he might have some ideas about other places to look or anyone local we should get in touch with."

Lola started the call to Mum, almost hoping she would be busy on a shout and she wouldn't be able to answer. She didn't want to be the one to tell Mum about Arlo. She didn't want to tell anyone. The more people who knew, the more it felt like Arlo really was gone.

"Hello, Dave! Is everything OK?" Mum sounded a bit surprised. Dad didn't often call her when she was at work.

"It's me," Lola told her. "I mean, it's Lola."

"Lola! Sweetheart, is something wrong?"

Lola felt tears burning at the back of her eyes and she swallowed hard before she answered. "We've lost Arlo. We can't find him anywhere, Mum. He's not in the house. And we've gone up and down the street looking but there's no sign of him."

"Oh, Lola… Oh no." Mum sounded really shaken. "Don't panic. I'm sure we'll find him. He'll come home when he's hungry, you know how much he loves his food."

"But what if he doesn't know where home is?" Lola asked. "He's not been outside since we got him, Mum. And nobody saw him on our road before he got stuck up that tree. He won't know where to go when he wants to go home!" She was really crying now, her voice wobbling and thick with tears. She didn't care that Noah was there, watching her.

"Cats are amazing, Lola, they're very clever," her mum said comfortingly. "There are all sorts of stories about cats finding their way home from the other side of the country. They've got a special instinct."

"Not when they're only kittens," Lola said – but she wanted her mum to tell her, yes, even when they were tiny kittens, even smaller than Arlo. That everything was going to be all right.

There was silence on the other end of the phone though, or almost silence. Just the faint chattering background noises of the fire station and her mum's soft breathing. She wasn't saying anything.

"Mum?" Lola whispered.

"Um, hang on a minute, Lola…"

Lola swallowed, trying to hold back her tears, but her breath kept coming in shaky gulps. She couldn't stop thinking about Arlo, hidden in a garden somewhere, or wandering along the pavement, trying to find his way back home.

"Are you OK?" Noah asked. He sounded embarrassed, as if he wasn't sure what to do with someone who definitely, obviously, wasn't OK. He lifted a hand as though he might pat her arm but then put it down again. "We'll keep looking," he said encouragingly. "Arlo's got to be here somewhere."

Lola lifted her head and stared down the empty street, and then looked meaningfully at Noah.

"He's got to be…" Noah murmured, but he didn't sound so cheerful now.

"Lola?" Mum was back on the phone now, and she sounded odd. She sounded as though she was trying not to laugh, Lola realized, feeling suddenly angry. This wasn't funny! How could Mum be laughing when Arlo was gone?

"Lola, you're never going to believe this… I was on the phone to you and I was leaning against the side of the fire engine, just by the driver's door. I've just sent you a photo. It'll be at the top of the screen, a little message icon. Have a look."

Lola took the phone away from her face and checked the screen – yes, there was a little message envelope. She clicked on it, and a photo appeared on the screen. The side of her mum's fire engine, with the door open so she could see into the cab. Lola could just see a bit of the front wheel, and the two red metal steps to get up inside. At the top of the steps, gazing worriedly into the camera, was a fluffy black kitten.

"Arlo!" Lola shrieked, so loud that she made Noah jump and he nearly fell over.

"What? Where?" He looked around wildly, thinking Lola had spotted him somewhere in the street.

"There!" Lola waved the phone at him. She was dancing up and down. "Mum, Mum, have you got him safe?" she demanded. "You're not leaving him in the fire engine, are you? Not with all that equipment – he'll climb everywhere, you know what he's like!"

"It's OK," her mum said, her voice low and soothing. It was the voice she used when Lola was getting worked up about something. "I've got him in the break room now. He's getting fussed over by everyone. Tim's going to make him a special second breakfast and we'll find a box or something to pop him in. He's looking quite happy. He

was a bit nervous when I first found
him, probably scared by all the noise.
The other crew hadn't long gone out
on a shout so it would have been very
loud for a little kitten."

"But – but how did he get there?"
Lola asked.

"That's what I've been trying to
work out. All I can think is that he
climbed into my backpack. I had it
in the kitchen while I was eating
breakfast this morning and you know
he likes climbing into little dark
spaces. If he got in there and went
to sleep, I might just have thrown
my door keys on top of my hoodie
and zipped it up – my fault for not
checking for stowaway kittens!"

"And he didn't wake up?" Lola asked

doubtfully. *She* would have woken up if someone dropped keys on top of her and carried her out to a car. Probably.

"Well, I guess not. He does sleep pretty deeply, doesn't he? Anyway, where's your dad? Hadn't you better tell him the news?"

"Oh! Yes. He's talking to Mr Khan from up the road. He was going to tell him that Arlo was missing." Lola laughed, feeling a bubble of happiness inside her.

"Can you ask him to come and pick Arlo up, please, love? I need to get on with work."

"I'll tell him. Bye, Mum! Look after Arlo!" Lola ended the call and beamed at Noah. "Come on, we've got to tell my dad!"

Lola dashed down the road to Mr Khan's house, where Dad was still chatting over the fence.

"Dad! Dad! Mum's got him! Arlo's at the fire station!"

Her dad swung round, staring at her, and Mr Khan stared too. "What are you talking about?" Dad said, bewildered. "How can he? It's miles away!"

"Mum thinks he climbed into her backpack," Lola explained, holding out the phone and showing Dad and Mr Khan the photo. Then she noticed another message icon at the top of the screen and opened it. This time the photo showed Arlo sitting on a table with a group of firefighters behind him, all making thumbs-up signs. "See?"

Mr Khan shook his head, laughing. "That kitten. He's an adventurer, yes? He's going to keep you busy."

"Mum says please can we go and get him?"

Dad shook his head. "Wow. Yes, of course. Let's go. Thanks for the help, Mr Khan – luckily I didn't need to call all those different shelters in the end!"

"Can I come?" Noah asked hopefully.

"I could go and ask my mum? I've never been to the fire station!"

"Oh, please, Dad!" Lola begged. "Noah was really kind helping us look."

"Fine by me, if your mum doesn't mind," Dad said. "You go and check with her, and then let's go get that kitten!"

Arlo could hear a voice that he knew. He edged out from underneath the driver's seat, so he could see through the open door. Lola's mum was there! She was talking to someone and she sounded worried.

He leaned out and padded his paw

on her sleeve, but she didn't notice,
so he patted her again, harder this time.
She stopped talking and glanced around
– and then her mouth fell open.

"Um, hang on a minute, Lola…"

She held the phone out for a
moment, pointing it at him, and then
she put it on the step and gently
reached in and scooped Arlo up,
holding him tight against her shirt.
She smelled like home, and like Lola
a little. Something that he knew,
at last. Arlo shut his eyes and purred.

Lola's mum went back to talking
but her voice had changed. It was
lighter and full of laughter. Something
had happened to make her happy,
Arlo thought wearily, listening as
she talked on.

"Shall we go and find you a treat?" Lola's mum murmured to him. "Come on, little one. Oh, Lola's been so upset about you…"

Dad, Lola and Noah hurried across the tarmac in front of the fire station. Lola had seen it once before – Mum had brought her there with Dad to have a look just before they'd moved – but she'd never been inside. There were huge glass and metal shutters across most of the front of the station, and she could see that one of the two fire engines was there behind them. A tall, smiling man was standing by the front doors, holding them open.

"Emma's family?" he asked, waving at them. "Come on through. We've got your little runaway in the break room."

He led them down a corridor to a room that looked a bit like a living room, with comfy chairs and sofas, and a table with a kettle and tea and coffee things. Curled up on the sofa, next to another firefighter, was a small black kitten, fast asleep.

"Arlo!" Lola breathed.

"We fed him a chopped-up sausage," the tall firefighter explained. "And after that it seemed like he was worn out. He just fell asleep on the sofa."

Lola crouched down by the sofa and gently stroked the top of Arlo's fluffy head. One greeny-yellow eye opened, peering sleepily at her, and then Arlo woke up properly. He staggered to his feet and began to march about on the sofa, purring and headbutting Lola lovingly every so often.

"We're going to have to check every bag that goes out of the house," Dad said, with a sigh. "Just in case there's a kitten in it."

The firefighter sitting on the sofa shook his head. "I don't think he'll fit in a bag for much longer. Not with the way he gobbled up that sausage."

"Here." The tall firefighter had disappeared out of the room and came back with two helmets, which he put on Lola and Noah. "Hold your kitten up, Lola, so I can take a photo. We need a record of our special visitor."

Arlo wriggled out of Lola's hands and clambered up on to her shoulder, sniffing at the strange helmet, and the firefighter laughed. "That's perfect. He'd make a great fire station mascot. I don't suppose you want to leave him with us?"

Lola could tell he was teasing but she still shook her head very firmly. Arlo was trying to burrow inside her hoodie now as if he wanted to get as close to her as he possibly could.

Lola unzipped the front a bit so he could snuggle in and held him there, with the soft fluff of his fur tickling against her neck. She could feel his purr, so big and loud that it was rumbling all through her.

Arlo might be a firefighter's kitten but he belonged with Lola.

HOLLY WEBB

Holly Webb started out as a children's
book editor and wrote her first series for
the publisher she worked for. She has been
writing ever since, with over one hundred
and fifty books to her name. Holly lives
in Berkshire, with her husband and three
children. Holly's pet cats are always
nosying around when she is trying
to type on her laptop.

For more information
about Holly Webb visit:

www.holly-webb.com